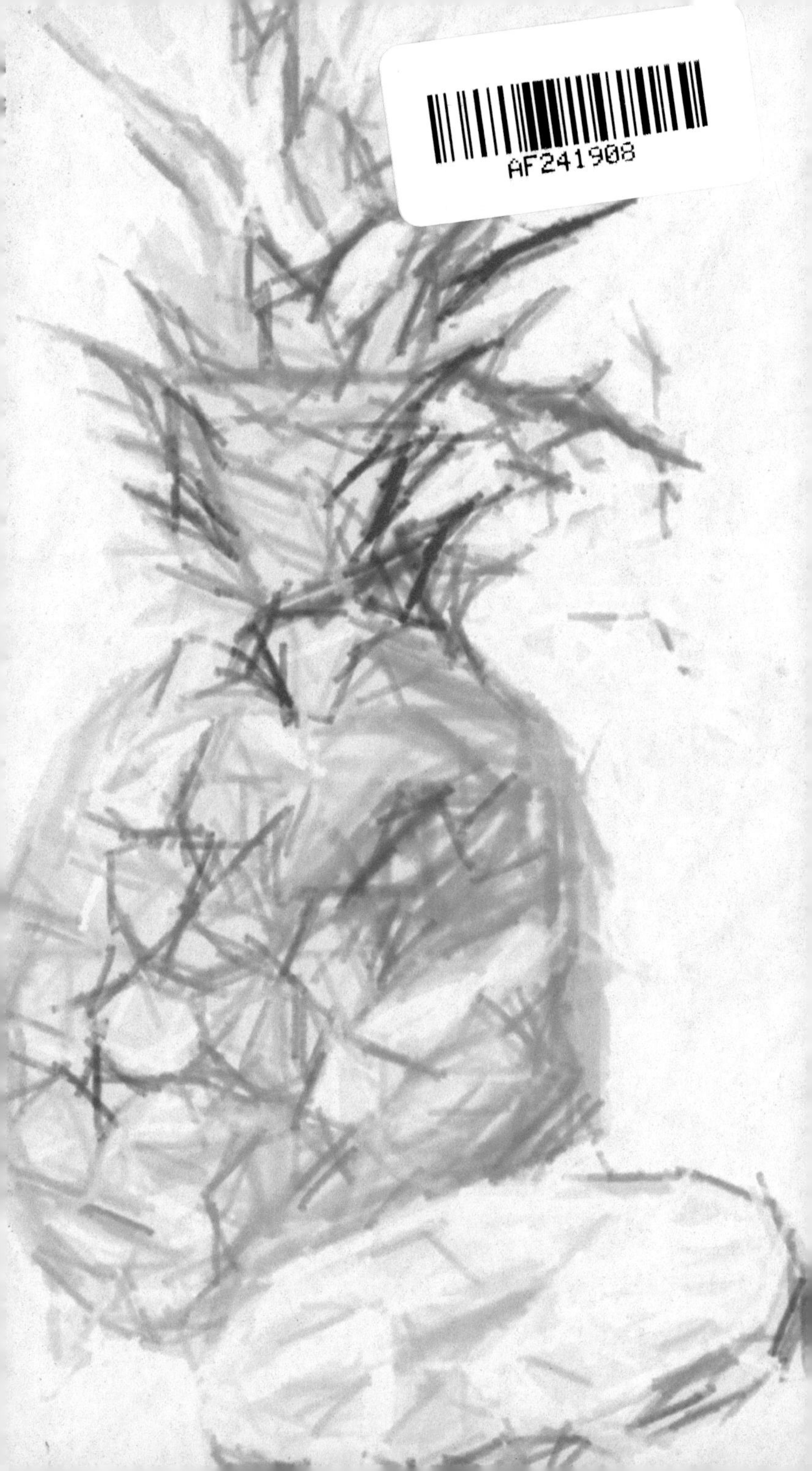
AF241908

Pineapple Dreams

Also by Aria Peyton

<u>Paranormal Romance</u>
Christmas Wishes
Witch Mate?
Taming the Menace

Coal Creek Shifters
#1 – *Entrusted*
#2 – *Encumbered*
#2.5 – *Enslaved*

<u>Contemporary Romance</u>
You Never Know

Aussie Dreams
Pineapple Dreams
Southern Dreams

<u>Supernatural</u>
Hell's Match
Cat (website only)

<u>Young Adult</u>
Oil & Water

Pineapple Dreams

ARIA PEYTON

Author's Note

It's been a while since this little tale was lucky enough to be one of six included in Hot Tree Publishing's *Going South* anthology in January 2017. I am forever grateful it was chosen among the multitudes that were submitted.

I've published it in a mini format that was small enough to fit in your pocket, and now I'm doing it in a size that will match the book that follows it: *Southern Dreams*.

I've only made minor corrections, so if you have a copy of *Going South*, or the postcard-sized version, you'll get exactly the same story here, only with another pretty cover!

Chapter One

I have a confession to make.

Yeah, I know, who doesn't, right? But please, hear me out.

My name's Belle. I'm freshly forty and have never been in love. Yep, you heard that right. Never. You'd think by this age I would have experienced true love. Well… no. I haven't.

At one point in my naïve and sexually undereducated life I thought I was… and then I fell pregnant and he left faster than Usain Bolt timed at the Olympics.

The stupid thing is, I wasn't even a teenager. I was twenty when this happened! But naïveté has no boundaries or age restrictions. If you don't know you're being played like a bloody fiddle, then shit is going to happen. In my case, shit hit in the form of twin girls two days after my twenty-first birthday, and you know what? Spending that milestone in extra-long labour is no fun at all.

So from twenty-one with newborns, to forty with nineteen-year-olds, I have travelled the rough road of single parenthood. For my birthday this year, I wanted to actually travel on proper roads and go somewhere. Anywhere. Preferably away from the stagnant little life I've found myself stuck in all these years.

Don't get me wrong, I love my girls to Jupiter and beyond, but there's something stifling about having an almost non-existent support base and no time for myself. None of this self-discovery business I've heard the other mums talk about over the years. No breaks. No holidays past the borders of South Australia. Nothing.

I'll tell you a little more about how my stupidity landed me in motherhood with no backup soon, but for now I'm on holiday with my girls. A joint birthday holiday out of the state—finally!—visiting iconic landmarks throughout some of our great country.

For years, I've wanted to travel overseas, take my girls on an adventure of cultures and landscapes. As you can imagine though, I've never managed to do this. By the time I had myself established in a job that paid enough to go travelling and accrue sufficient annual leave, my girls had reached high school and their hellish study load. I felt guilty for wanting to take them away from everything for a few months and have them miss out on their education—despite the excellent learning they could've done while trekking around another country.

Time whittled away like wood under a knife, until this year. With my fortieth birthday looming, and my twins, Ronni and Chrissy—Veronica and Christabel on official documents—about to start university after taking a gap year to get out there and work, I wanted to finally grab life by the balls and go somewhere, experience something different, let my hair down for a change.

Grasping at straws, and possibly the last opportunity I may ever have to travel with my children, I decided to plan a holiday for us. A trip around part of Australia to see as many *big* things as we could.

So here we are, spending the summer holidays on a road trip through Oz. When we first started out, Ronni scoffed at what I had planned for us, and Chrissy gave me the biggest eyeroll I've ever witnessed, so large I'm surprised she didn't manage to see her own brain back there. Despite their occasional protests though, I can see their secret enjoyment in our trip. I mean seriously, what's not to love about a giant turnbuckle and propeller?

We've been through Victoria, New South Wales, and crossed the border into Queensland to spend a couple of weeks seeing every big thing we can. In addition, we've been to Australia Zoo to appease Chrissy and her love of animals, and we've seen as many art galleries as we can find to soothe the artist in Ronni.

But as we come closer to needing to make the journey home again, we're spending our final week in Woombye, the home of the Big Pineapple, as well as the Big Macadamia. Yum to both of those! And it's just our luck that a gallery, Queensland Zoo, and the pineapple are in walking distance of each other, and all are nice and close to the caravan park we're staying in. It's my pleasure to be able to indulge them both in what they love.

We cruise the town after settling into our caravan. It's easy to tell we're tourists from the southern end of the country. Everyone around us is tanned and buff. Okay, maybe not everyone, but certainly the local contingent we're paying attention to. Although our pasty white skin has finally browned a little on our road trip, it's still very obvious that we're not from around here.

We attract attention with the combination of our almost vampiric paleness and very clear burn lines. All right, I'll be honest, my *girls* attract the attention. They're young, gorgeous, and have sass. I'm just the frumpy-looking mum who never had the time to regain her pre-baby body no matter how hard she tried.

But that's okay. Kind of. All right, so I'm learning to accept it.

Instead of worrying though, I enjoy the view from behind my mirrored sunnies of all the hot young studmuffins who openly perv on my teens. I'm glad they're nineteen; otherwise the urge to bitch-slap some of these guys would be stronger than it is now. Anyone under twenty-five can perv… okay, maybe thirty is the *absolute* max, but over that and it just gets skeezy.

Especially the ones clearly over the hill or with their wives. I glare over the top of my sunglasses at them.

At dinnertime on our first evening in town, we sit outside a small but noisy restaurant-slash-café in the centre of town, enjoying the prospect of dinner and the still-warm air of summer. When our waiter comes around, it's my turn to feel like the skeezy perv. Or am I allowed to claim cougar status now?

My skin tingles with awareness as he stands next to me and hands out the small menus. His voice resonates within me when he reads out the daily specials, a smile on his face the whole time. The urge to kiss that smile surges through me, taking me by surprise. I thrust my hands beneath the table, gripping the chair tight to keep from launching myself at this unsuspecting young man.

As he smiles again and walks off, I realise I have absolutely no idea what the specials are. I heard none of the words, only the timbre and cadence of his voice. My view of his arse as he walks back through the door to serve someone else wavers when Ronni grabs hold of my shoulder and shakes the crap out of me.

"Mum. Mum! Yoo-hoo. Over here, space cadet."

I wrench my eyes away from the hunk who I hope will be back soon and glare at Chrissy first for her smartarse words, and at Ronni for shaking me.

"Do you mind?"

Ronni snorts. "Geez, Mum. Feel free to perv all you like, but do you think you can be a little bit subtle about it next time? You were starting to drool."

Chrissy snort-laughs—a snaughle—from the other side of the table, earning another scowl.

"Was not," I grumble, surreptitiously wiping my lower lip. Just in case. This makes them laugh harder. I love being the brunt of their humour some days. Makes me feel freaking awesome. My inner sarcastic bitch is flipping them the bird as I shoot mummy daggers across the table to them. I may be forty, but I can still stoop to their level of immaturity at a moment's notice.

With a "Hmph" I pick up a menu and scan what's listed. But that's all I manage to do. Scan. Nothing sticks in my head because all I can see floating across the page is a set of magnificent blue eyes, the kind I long to stare into as I ride the owner into the sunset. I allow my thoughts to wander under the sheets, a fantasy never to come true, until I'm rudely shaken out of it. Again!

"What?" I snap at Ronni. Chrissy snaughles again and tries unsuccessfully to muffle it with her napkin. I pin each daughter with a stare, watching as their identical faces fill with mirth. "What's so fucking funny, you twits?"

Chrissy loses it laughing, pointing slightly to my right with one hand as the other slaps the table. I turn slowly, feeling the increase in tingles as I meet his gaze. His cerulean eyes are crinkled with his smile as he so obviously fights the urge to join my daughters in their chuckle fest. I want to glare at him too, just for taking their side, so I slide my sunnies down the bridge of my nose and pin him with *the look* every mother perfects when their children are young.

The intention to laugh leaves his face, his lips no longer stifling humour. Instead, he unconsciously licks the bottom one. The crinkles leave the corners of his eyes, only to be replaced by dilated pupils and a look I've only read about. But dammit, the moment is broken when Chrissy coughs rather loudly.

"I'd like to order the fettuccine carbonara, please, with a side salad, and a vodka raspberry."

Mr Smooth and Delectable nods, not breaking eye contact for extended seconds until Chrissy coughs again, this time with a laugh in it. Something flashes in his gorgeous eyes; regret, maybe? He taps in her order on his iPad and turns to Ronni. She orders too, and then all eyes are on me.

Fuck! I hadn't taken in anything from the menu, didn't hear the specials before, and have no clue what to order.

"And what can I get for you?" His sultry voice shivers through me, and as I open my mouth to give him a sassy answer, I find myself tongue-tied and stuttering. I swallow, trying to force the words from my throat to order my dinner. With a shake of my head, I grab my water, take a large gulp, and hang my head in dismay. I can't even speak around him. This is ridiculous!

Finally, I manage to croak, "What would you recommend?"

His smile lightens the pressure on my throat, and as he speaks, enticing me with promises of delicious morsels of food, my imagination runs wild, hearing that same voice make vows of hot nights and even hotter sex.

"That sounds great," I murmur, forcing the words past lips gone dry again. "Thank you."

I'm lost in thoughts of our to-die-for waiter when the object of my daydreams returns to the table, laden with plates.

"Your orders, ladies," he announces in his velvet tones. I can't help but glance up at him over the rims of my glasses, meeting his eyes as he places my plate down. He drags a smile from me with his own grin, then walks off inside. By the time I turn back to the table, Ronni is already scoffing her dinner and Chrissy is inspecting hers.

With my fork in hand, I look down, hand poised to dig in. "What's this?"

My girls stop midchew and frown at me. "Wha ou mean?" Ronni garbles through a mouthful. "Ou ord'd ee."

"Yes, I know I ordered it. But what in the hell did I order?" I'm staring at the colourful mess on my plate in confusion. "Surely you have some idea of what this is."

Chrissy giggles through her food, then swallows before replying, "I think it was some kind of new-age fried rice. I think… I can't be quite sure. I was too busy watching you drooling over the waitstaff to take any notice of your food choice."

I can't help the scowl I aim her way, muttering, "Well you're no bloody help, then."

Ronni laughs as she wipes her lips on a napkin. "Pretty sure it's fancy veggie rice, Mum. But I have to admit, you were funnier to watch than to listen to him speak."

"Speak for yourself. I found his voice —"

"We get it. Mesmerising." I watch them drag out the word and make funny faces at me, rolling their eyes in an "I'm under hypnosis" type motion. Dickheads. I bred dickheads, seriously.

"Shut up, both of you." For anyone observing this table, I wouldn't blame them for thinking I wasn't their mother. I can't help the smile I'm hiding though. They really do act more like friends at times than my kids. I like the banter I'm able to share with them.

We eat in between comfortable silences and pleasant conversation. The food is delicious and despite my initial shock at not knowing what the hell was on my plate, I'm glad I went with his recommendation.

"How do you two feel about dining here tomorrow night?" I ask casually, popping another mouthful in and chewing slowly. I studiously avoid eye contact.

"Oh yeah, sure, Mum. That sounds great. Any particular reason you don't want to try another fine dining establishment?" There's humour in Chrissy's voice.

I wave my fork around airily. "No reason other than the food here is great. Thought we might try something different on the menu tomorrow."

Chrissy shakes her head at me as she scoops up her last forkful and points it at me, one eye squinting. "We're onto you, you know that, right?"

Giving her my "I'm totally innocent" look, I shake my head. "No idea." But there's a smirk there for her. We laugh together and are still laughing when Mr Voice of Velvet comes back to collect our plates.

"How was your meal, ladies?"

At our nods, he smiles briefly at my girls, and a little longer at me, before gathering the dishes. "Can I get you a dessert menu at all?"

Although the offer is tempting, and I really could do with some sweets, I glance around the table before speaking. "No, thanks. Not tonight." I grace him with a smile and hope to hell he's on tomorrow night.

"Tomorrow, perhaps?"

I receive a blinding grin in response, which makes my chest flutter. I'm almost 100 percent sure I'm not having a heart attack, but something's going on in there. I nod once, struggling to look away from him.

When he leaves and our table is clean of everything but our drinks, Ronni slaps my arm, whisper-yelling, "He was *so* flirting with you, Mum!"

"Huh? What?" I'm gobsmacked. But if anyone is going to know what flirting is, it's my girls. I think they mastered the art in order to get their own way, score discounts in shops, and who knows what else, so I'm leaning toward believing her claim. "Really?" The blush that steals up my cheeks can't be stopped, so when he comes back with the bill, I'm bright freaking red. I just nod mutely at him.

"See! Totally flirting with you." Chrissy joins in the declaration. She looks at Ronni and they share their silent twin speak. They both nod and turn to me. "Okay, we'll come back tomorrow night. I'm curious to see where this goes."

Chapter Two

The next day we get up early and go shopping at Sunshine Plaza. We all have a ball and spend way too much money, but it's so worth being able to kick back and relax about it for a change. We have lunch at Maroochy Surf Club, then stroll up the beach towards Cotton Tree, checking out the cool rock formations embedded in the sand.

I still have no idea what they are, but they look amazing. The views from my map app are even better than on the ground. Gotta love technology. Time flies by as we enjoy the sand between our toes and the wind in our hair. Naturally, Ronni complains that she'll have to wash the seawater out of her hair, but really, girl, live a little already!

It's past five when we set out on the return journey, and the girls fidget in their seats as we near Woombye. It's annoying me, all the constant wriggle and jiggle in the car.

"What's up? You two got worms or something?"

Chrissy snorts and shakes her head at me in the rearview mirror. "Nup. Just wanna get to dinner."

I squint one eye at her in the mirror. "Oh yeah. And why's that?" I try to fight my smile at the prospect of seeing the spunky waiter again as I wait for her answer.

"I think you know why, Mum. I think you'd be jiggling too if you weren't driving."

Ronni chimes in with, "I wanna see if Mr Flirty ups his game tonight."

I can hear the laughter in their voices, and it makes me smile even as it sort of hurts. I can count on one hand how many times I've dated while they've been on this planet. And that's kind of sad if you think about it. It's a wonder my pink parts haven't cobwebbed over by now. And it's not for lack of trying either.

My darling daughters have tried to set me up with single dads, teachers, after-school carers, police officers, and anyone else they can think of who might date an on-the-larger-side mother of two. Coffee with whoever their choice of the week was has been about the extent of it, with only a few making it to an actual date. It makes me sigh, but I've resigned myself to being alone in this life.

That is until Mr Hot Stuff at the restaurant popped on by. Now my neglected pussy is craving some attention and responding intensely to him alone.

Which is a shame because, even without asking, I know he's too young. And why the hell would he be interested, anyway? I dined with two very gorgeous young women last night who are obviously much closer to his age bracket. I hate that I'm suddenly jealous of my own daughters, but I can't lie and say I haven't wished a time or two to be that young again and actually able to have fun.

My hands grip the steering wheel as I fight the surge of emotion those thoughts bring. I wouldn't give up my girls for the world, but I'm allowed to wish I'd been a little more experienced and knowledgeable about such things before throwing my social life to the wind so early. I'm entitled to not want to be lonely for the rest of my life.

The café comes into view, making me wonder how I got us here in one piece when I wasn't paying any attention to where I was driving. I give myself a mental pat on the back for us all being alive, then find a car park nearby. We head into the café and find a seat outside again, quietly hoping we get the same waiter.

I'm not disappointed, and I think Ronni and Chrissy are pretty happy too. The smirks on their faces are damn obvious, their hands and curtained hair not hiding a bloody thing. I'm scowling at them as they giggle like ten-year-olds before I realise that there's heat emanating from someone beside me. I turn slowly, craning my neck up as I do.

It's him. He managed to get the menus on the table without me noticing. The smile on his lips makes my insides go gooey as our eyes meet. This man, as young and unattainable as he is, creates sensations within me that I'm not familiar with; the types of feelings I've only ever imagined from reading second-hand romance novels on the bus to work each day now buzz through me. They spark heat and longing in areas thought long dead from disuse.

"Good evening, ladies. What can I start you off with tonight?" His velvet voice winds its way through my centre, undoing any semblance of poise I'd retained.

"Midori lemonade for me, please. Girls?"

"Vodka raspberry for me," Chrissy says, while Ronni orders a tequila sunrise.

"Sheesh, Ron, you planning on walking or rolling out of here tonight?" Chrissy asks her.

"Ha. Ha. Mum's driving, so I'm good to go."

I suck in air at her words, unnoticed by them as they laugh it up and start a conversation I tune out. I don't want to see the look on our waiter's face now, knowing that he is privy to our relationship. A feather-light touch on my arm snags my attention back to him, and he gives me a small smile. "I'll be back shortly with your drinks."

Disappointment fills me as he walks off to do his job. The angle of the sunlight catches on his tanned skin, highlighting the structure of his toned arms. I get a tiny peek through his work shirt as he moves, but it's so brief. I sigh at the impossible dream of having someone young and insanely good-looking being interested in me. Focusing my attention on the menu, I slip off into a world where love exists for me and I'm deliriously happy.

My girls pick up on my melancholy and order for me when he returns. I hear them asking for his recommendation like I did last night, so I'm sure to get another random dish for dinner. I can feel him hovering next to me, almost like he wants me to look up, but I can't. It hurts to be affected so much by someone so out of reach. Even the kick to the shins by one of my traitorous daughters doesn't budge me.

Dinner takes time, the crowd tonight being larger than last night, but it flies as my teens drag me into their conversation, chipping away at my misery. Before we know it, plates are being placed down on the table in front of Ronni and Chrissy. They glance at me briefly and dig in, hunger overriding the need to be polite, it seems. By the time I look up, he's gone again. I listen to a conversation had through mouths full of food, shaking my head at their manners, or lack thereof.

As I'm contemplating if these teens really are mine, a plate is set gently before me. A finger runs lightly over my arm and lingers, not actually leaving my skin. I can't help but look up this time.

"Enjoy," he tells me. There's still a smile there, lingering on his lips, but it seems not as bright as before, not as blinding. I push my sunglasses to the top of my head, snagging them in my hair, and meet his eyes. The contact seems to last a lifetime, when in reality it's probably mere seconds. His smile strengthens, in turn bolstering my own. The resting finger near my wrist strokes ever so gently, creating a concentrated spot of burning heat.

That finger sneaks down toward my own, and as I shift my hand to pick up my knife, I lift my pinkie slightly. There's tiny contact as his finger wraps around mine, a minute amount of time where the universe aligns for me.

And then the moment is over as he gives my pinkie a squeeze and turns away from the table, returning to his job. If I wasn't seated already, I'd likely swoon as he glances back from the café's doorway, shooting another smile my way. I pick up my drink and have a sip through the straw as I watch him until he disappears from sight. When I turn my attention back to the table, I'm being stared at.

"Well, I think that answers that one, Chris," Ronni announces, picking up her cocktail and slurping it. My cringe is automatic. "I do believe that our darling mother is being hit on." Her grin is huge and apparently contagious, as Chrissy's face splits into a smile, too.

"I do believe you're right, Ronni dear. What are we going to do about this?"

At that, I freak out slightly. "Do? You'll do nothing. Every time you've attempted to set me up with someone before, it never worked."

"You ended up screwing the cop, didn't you?" Ronni mutters, at the same time Chrissy speaks again.

"Awww, come on, Mum. Besides, if we *do* nothing this time, then you'll end up *doing* no one. Again."

I raise an eyebrow at her, earning me her patented puppy/kitten eyes. Puppy dog eyes were never enough for her; she had to go and combine it with sad kitty eyes. The result is disturbing when you want to stand your ground. But I need to. They're dabbling in my life here, and if I'm going to fuck up this opportunity, whatever it may be, then it's going to be *my* fuck-up, not theirs.

I hold up a finger, halting her words but not her expression. It's pathetic, but in the funniest way. I can't help myself, I crack up laughing. And that laughter manages to attract attention. I really should learn to laugh quieter, but I just can't. It's big, it kind of booms, and it's definitely not for the faint of heart. But you know what? Tonight I just don't care. I couldn't give a shit if my laugh is big, or if people are looking over. I'm finally having fun with my children, my gorgeous nineteen-year-old girls, and living without restrictions.

It's such a freeing revelation!

And then, from inside the café, comes the man who makes me dare to dream again. The nameless waiter with gorgeous everything. As he serves the other tables outside, he gifts me with little glances, the occasional flick of his eyes in my direction. Even if this is just a bit of fun flirting, it gives me the hope that one day I'll find my happily ever after like most people dream of. If nothing else, he's given me hope.

Chapter Three

The next morning I awake from dreams of our nameless waiter, a flash of arousal engulfing my tired body. In the years of unintentional celibacy, I've done my fair share of "rubbing one out." Now is one of those times when I wish I could do just that. But… kids. A scowl pulls at my eyebrows as my heated core cries out for attention. I desperately need relief.

Pushing back the sheet, I make an early trip to the bathroom, doing my business before jumping in for a shower. Wasting no time, I lather up and reach between my legs.

Showered and a damn sight more relaxed than when I woke, I break out the map of the town. Today we're going to the Big Pineapple. It's the perfect location really, since Queensland Zoo is on the same plot of land, and the art gallery too. We'll all be happy Vegemites in one trip. The last time I visited was when I was nine. It holds memories I've always wanted to rekindle.

I guess it's time to see if those memories hold up to the reality of now.

Everyone is up, showered, breakfasted, and ready to roll, so we head out. I don't think I've mentioned it yet, but we've cruised in classic luxury on this road trip. When my dad passed away, he left me his Ford XY GT sedan. I think it was his way of saying sorry for ditching me when I needed him most. It's in pristine condition and runs like a dream. The V8 engine rumbles like nobody's business, and chews through petrol like you wouldn't believe.

Off we go, thundering along the highway to the parking lot across from the iconic pineapple. It's already hot by midmorning and I can feel the sweat rolling down my back beneath my bra strap as we cross the overpass, watching the cars whizz along beneath our feet.

My admiration of the Big Pineapple is scoffed at by Chrissy, who just wants to get to the zoo. "All in good time," I tell her as I walk towards it. First on my agenda is to ride the plantation train before the heat becomes any worse. "Come on, let's go for a ride!"

I pay the money at the café counter and we find our way through to the platform where the train departs. I love it when I time things just right. We look out over the plantation while we wait.

"Are you going to climb the pineapple when we get back, Mum?" Chrissy asks.

With my insane vertigo at the damn Big Rocking Horse, her question is a reasonable one. "Yeah, why the hell not. I did that blasted horse. Nothing's going to stop me from climbing a pineapple." I grin at them both as the train pulls up and passengers disembark. An announcement rattles through speakers nearby. The voice is strangely familiar, but the distortion from the speakers and the noise from the passengers heading back inside make it hard to distinguish.

The next half hour is spent enjoying the up and down of the track, the rainforest, passing the zoo, and all the sights in between. I'm happily hot and a little windblown on our return, and eager to climb to the top viewing platform of the landmark structure.

Photos are taken, selfies are posted online, and we

enjoy the tiny space as we look out as far as we can see. The breeze up here is cooling, and I put off descending the stairs as long as I can. Eventually though, thirst gets the better of me and I give in, going down to see about lunch in their café.

As we step out into the sunshine, I misjudge my footing, miss the last step, and stumble heavily, making a freaking spectacle of myself in front of strangers. I was always told not to worry about the opinions of others, but it's hard not to when people are staring at you like you're some kind of clumsy freak.

"Oh shit, Mum, are you okay?" Ronni is at my side in a flash, making sure I'm steady on my feet before she lets me go and steps back to assess the damage.

"I'm fine, Ronni, just a stupid trip."

"You almost fell on your arse, Mum. No stupid trip about it." Guiding me towards the gift shop and café, she starts brushing me down as if I were covered in dust and dirt. I'm forty and suddenly embarrassed by my child touching my butt in public.

"Oh my God, Ronni, can you stop that, please? I never hit the ground so there's nothing to dust off." She keeps going. "Get your hands off my butt, Ron!"

She laughs at me, continuing with her inappropriate touching. People are watching her as they come and go, curiosity in some gazes, humour in others.

I blush, wanting to crawl inside a hole. Embarrassment floods me as my face burns, the red hue creeping from my chest all the way to my damn eyebrows. As I'm dying from mortification, I hear a familiar masculine chuckle nearby. *Oh God! It's him!* That makes it even worse. My hands shoot up to cover my face, hiding from the hot waiter of the past two nights.

Ronni hits me across the bicep, sending my arm fat wobbling, increasing the wish for the ground to open and swallow me whole. Although, at the rate I'm going, I'll get stuck in the crevice and never get out in either direction.

I slide the brim of my cap further down over my eyes and wait for the clock to speed up, taking me out of this moment and into tomorrow. Of course, the universe doesn't hear my desperate plea. I know this from the excited yet hushed whispers coming from my two teens. It's a wonder they're not giggling maniacally. For the first time ever, I wish I could shrink like a cock in cold water.

"Are you okay there, ma'am?" His voice may be steady but I can see the damn smirk, and ma'am? *Really?* I groan at the same time Chrissy snickers.

"Ma'am. He called Mum ma'am!" They both lose it in a fit of hysteria, leaving me floundering before the hottest guy I've had the pleasure of meeting in… well, ever. I have the overwhelming urge to slap them both, but I'm sure that'll look like grand parenting in front of the hot stranger. At least I find my voice this time.

"Ugh. Don't mind them. Teenage freaks."

His deep chuckle sends those zings of something I haven't experienced down my spine. The more he laughs, the farther it travels. His voice at the café was one thing but oh my, that chuckle is another monster entirely. In minutes, my body is humming and all I want to do is lie down and ride the feeling to its natural end. Without warning, the laughing stops, from both my girls and the man who makes me sizzle.

Slowly, I peel my eyes open—*when the hell did I shut them?*—and actually take notice of what's going on around me. My girls are staring at me like I've got two heads, and *he* is giving me a *look*. His eyes are hooded and the slight smirk on his lips is making the tingle deepen.

"What?" I ask, looking between the three of them. Chrissy shakes her head, eyes rolling like I'm dense, while Ronni crosses her arms over her damn perky boobs, grinning like an idiot. It'd be nice to have perky boobs again. I want to scowl at my stupid thoughts, but as my eyebrows dip, a light touch on my shoulder sends my heart racing.

"Nothing, ma'am. You look a little flustered though. Would you like to sit down for a bit?"

Mortification threatens to rise and laugh at my clumsiness, but is squashed by the glance Mr Doable gives me. It's different from the expressions he gave me at the café, and I can't quite decipher it. However, it seems my daughters already have. Despite their giggles and eyerolls, when I turn back to them, gesturing for them to follow me, their wide eyes and shooing motions tell another story. Frowning, I mouth, "What?" Chrissy gives me her well-practised head shake, the one meant to tell me I'm an idiot, and strides over to me.

"Mum, he's hot, he's still eyeing you off, and offering for you to *sit down*. For fuck's sake, just go already!"

Her demanding whisper encourages one of my eyebrows to lift in question, earning me yet another eyeroll. Practically shoving me away, she takes a few steps back and crosses her arms again, foot tapping impatiently on the rough-sawn wooden floorboards. Seeing my indecision, Ronni flaps her hands at me too, the shooing motion reminiscent of trying to fend off mozzies.

I relent and turn away, checking over my shoulder that they'll be okay. By the time I turn, they're both giggling, heads together, shooting me looks and hand waves to move me along. Then they turn their attention to what's on the shelf in front of them, having already found some quirky souvenir I'll no doubt be buying them later. As I face the front to see where I'm going—since bashing into something now would be the icing on the cake—I see Mr Spunky waiting for me by a door behind the register.

As I pass customer service, he touches the small of my back, guiding me through the door. I can't help the involuntary flinch as his hand sends heat through me. He must feel my movement, because he withdraws the contact and the tingles stop. My shoulders sag and my head drops, along with any self-esteem I'd managed to regain by his apparent interest in me.

The seat against the wall looks comfy and I drop myself onto it, uncaring at this point of my life whether I appear elegant or like a heifer. With a quick flick, I drop my handbag to the floor and lean my head right back across the low backrest, resting it against the wall. When I take my hat off, hair sticks to my face with the incredible humidity here in Queensland, and I can imagine I look like a hot mess.

Great.

I finally manage to get in a small space with a hot male for the first time in *years* and I probably look like shit. Story of my fekking life.

Chapter Four

I hear plastic snap and lift my head too fast from the wall, cracking my neck in the process. The world spins before me as my eyes adjust. Mr Spunkytrunks is offering me a bottle of water, the condensation on the outside showing me that it's icy cold and ready for gulping. Without any decorum, my grabby hands snatch the bottle and bring it to my forehead, rolling the cold plastic over my sweat-sticky skin.

The heat today makes me wonder why in the ever-loving fuck I brought us here in summer. Of all times of the year, bloody summer. Idiot!

With my eyes closed, I smooth the cold, condensation-wet bottle over my face and down my neck. A soft groan escapes me at the cooling sensation, which seems to elicit a slightly louder groan from the young man I'd almost forgotten is with me. *Ha!* That's total bullshit; I knew he was there. Slowly opening my eyes, I have to confess that I like what I see standing nearby.

As I continue to roll the cold bottle over my neck and top of my chest, I take in the fine specimen of masculinity that gives me tingles. Bronze from the Queensland sun, muscles galore adorning his sculpted biceps and pecs, and thighs that look like they could support… ahem… well, they look sturdy. His shorts hug those thighs, giving me a better look at the legs. I avoid glancing at the bulge for now.

I allow my eyes to scan farther down, coming to rest

on the tattoos winding around his calves. A dragon curls its head around the right leg just under his knee, a foreleg and claws resting beneath its chin.

A husky chuckle brings my eyes slowly back up his body, not missing an inch of the delicious-looking man. The glint in his eyes and the smile gracing his lips brings that tingle up to a burn. He licks those lips as they roll in and out, a cheeky smile appearing on the glistening, kissable... *No!* Must not think any more dirty thoughts about—

"Like what you see?"

His voice. Oh my God, his voice does it for me every time he speaks. It's like chocolate-smothered cheesecake. Meeting his eyes, I can't control the slight nod. *Traitorous head!* And it seems that my tongue is in on the mutiny as it peeks out to wet my own lips, dry despite the water... which is still in my hand. Without breaking eye contact, I twist the cap off the bottle and gulp the cold water. It soothes the parched walls of my throat, the chill refreshing as it cools the burning desire within me.

Or at least I can wish it does. All it really does is give me a brain freeze.

Within seconds of guzzling almost a full bottle of ice-cold water, my head is throbbing and searing pain shoots through my temples.

"Ah fuck!" I swear, clutching my head as I shake it from side to side. "Fuck a fucking duck!" My foot joins in, stomping on the wooden floor, sending echoes bouncing in the small room. "The pain, the pain!" See, this is why I stay away from Slurpees and shit like that these days; I just have no damn tolerance for the things I used to. Damn aging sucks balls.

As I'm in the death throes of a massive head freeze,

warm hands slip in under mine and a whispered "I've been dreaming of this for two days" feathers across my cheek before lips make contact with mine. Their caress is gentle, trialling the contact, but as the desire flaming through me increases, the head chill wanes and my passion kicks in. He must sense when I'm good to go, as the movement of his lips becomes less gentle, more urgent.

A groan vibrates in my mouth as my fingers tug on his hair. *When did my hands sneak in there?*

Who cares; the strands are long enough to grab, and smooth to the touch. I tug again, enjoying the effect it has on his kissing. Unable to help myself, I nibble on his bottom lip, tugging the stubble-edged flesh between my teeth.

Unlike previous men, this guy seems to like my lip nibbles and it spurs him on. The kiss becomes deeper, more passionate, and I suddenly find myself pulled up out of my seat and pressed hard against him. Hands are on my ample butt, pushing me closer to his ripped body, my soft and squishy to his hard and oh… *hard*. Swoon. Instinct has me grinding, pushing my pelvis as close to his as I can manage.

It's divine!

His fingers squeeze my arse, and mine are on their way to return the favour when a loud bang has us both jerking back. I lose balance, falling backwards into the chair, hair mussed, legs akimbo, and shooting daggers at the person who dared interrupt the first decent kiss I've had in bloody years.

The interrupter glares straight back, tapping her foot on the floor and her finger on the watch on her wrist. Ronni huffs impatiently at me.

"You've had your fun, Mum. Now it's time to go. You

promised we'd go to the art gallery today, and Chrissy wants to talk to the keepers at the zoo. It's getting bloody hot out there and—"

I'm gobsmacked. Utterly speechless. "Your timing sucks nuts, kid." The chair has decided to keep me, as when I try to haul my arse out of it, I just can't. I may have turned to jelly under the caress of expert lips. After several failed attempts, with my daughter waiting in the doorway, arms crossed, and Spunky McHard-on still standing in front of me, I huff in frustration and blow the sticky strands of hair out of my face.

Or at least I try to. Those fuckers aren't going anywhere in a hurry.

Crossing one leg over the other, I fold my arms over my large bosom and lean back. "Well, I guess you'll be waiting a while, Ronni. This chair doesn't want me to go anywhere." I give her one of my patented "mum" smiles; you know what I mean—the one that tells you you're not going to get anywhere by arguing with me at this very moment.

Rough pads gently stroke along the back of my arm, following the line of my forearm to my hand. His fingers curl around my own, linking them together. With a firm tug and mesmerising stare, he yanks me up out of the possessive chair until I'm standing right up against him. When I go to move away, he holds firm to my hand, stopping me in my tracks. I frown at him, trying again to leave.

All I get is a small shake of his head. His eyes move to the door and back to me. Repeats. I turn my head. "Ronni, take a twenty out of my purse and grab what you and your sister want from the shop." I shuffle my handbag towards her with my foot from where it sits on the floor. "Grab a couple of cold drinks too and meet me outside somewhere shady."

"You're shady at the moment, Mum," Ronni mumbles as she bends down to retrieve a twenty-dollar note from my purse. I feel my bag hit my ankle as she slings it back over to me, and the door soon shuts behind her.

Fingers thread through my damp hair and down my cheek. "Where were we?" he asks. After being crashed back into reality, I try to pull away from him, regretful that I have to leave, but also aware of the certainty that this isn't anything more than a delightful kiss on a summer's afternoon. A frown dips his brow when he sees my reluctance.

"Why so sad, pretty lady?"

"My name's Belle, and I'm no pretty lady." My voice is sad; there's no hiding it. He strokes my cheek again, thumb coming down to play across my bottom lip. I almost swoon at his touch, but I don't. Steeling my legs, I try to sidestep, but end up tripping on my bag instead. Down we go, me onto my fleshy butt, back hitting the floor hard, and the taut-muscled hottie landing perfectly in line with my hot and tingly lady parts.

For an accident, it couldn't have been planned better if I'd tried. Except I really have to go and I don't want to. I can hear my girls' voices outside the door, chatting to the other people in the shop serving the pineapple-shaped tourist trap.

"I have to go…." I look at him pointedly, wanting to know his name.

"Matt. My name's Matt." His lips are so close when he speaks, breath skating over my mouth. I want to bite those lips again, and they're so damn near. Near enough for catching.

My thoughts are lost in a trance as I pull my torso up

off the floor to capture his mouth with mine. Arms wrap around my upper back, keeping me off the floor, and I reciprocate, wrapping mine around under his arms to clasp at his rippling muscles. If I had claws, they'd be deeply imbedded in Matt's shoulders right about now, and most likely needing a pair of pliers to be removed.

The kiss ends naturally this time, no interruptions by cock-blocking daughters. Speaking of which....

"I know I'd probably have your balls if you'd tried, but why in the hell weren't you trying to pick up my girls instead of me?"

Mouth working its way down my neck, he murmurs, "I'm not one for younger girls. Always had an eye for an older woman, but I can't have done too well this time with such a small gap between us."

"Flattery will get you everywhere," I gasp as he nibbles my throat. "But I think you're too young for me, Matt."

He lifts up, shaking his head at me. "I don't think so. Doesn't matter anyway. Age is irrelevant in the long run. Just passion and the commitment people share."

This conversation is getting deeper than I'm comfortable with. I may have had a hot make-out session with him, but I don't know Matt and he doesn't know me. I wriggle beneath him, feeling his erection pressing my hot spot. Dammit! I'm throbbing down there, ready for action. It's been so damn long.

I stop moving and meet his eyes. "I need to get up. My girls and I have places to go. It was nice to meet you, Matt." I manage to work my arms up from where they're wedged and hold one hand under his nose, palm out for a friendly shake. He glances at my hand and back to my eyes. His crinkle with amusement, as if I've done something funny, and instead of taking my hand in his, he dips his head and sucks on a finger.

Fireworks shoot through me at the erotic contact, sending my pelvis into another fit of unconscious grinding against his cock. His suction gets stronger and a moan escapes him. I'm so rooted! No matter what this guy does to me, he sets my body aflame. It's enough to drive any sane woman to the nuthouse. Teeth drag up my fingertip until he reaches the top, letting it go gently.

He leans in to kiss my nose and backs off, kneeling before me and offering me a hand with which to haul myself off the floor. When we're upright once more, I hold out my hand in the gesture I was aiming at just a minute ago.

"It really was nice to meet you, Matt. That was, um, fun." I plaster a smile on my face to cover up the disappointment trying to crowd in. Fun is fun, and usually never lasts. Unless it results in children; then the fun stays with you always.

I push aside the past and take a step back from what I wish was my future. My wayward thoughts have me stumbling but before he can help me, I've righted myself and am bending to grab my handbag from the floor. "I'm fine. Just a bit wobbly. Nothing new." I'm babbling and need to get out of here. Fast. Before I do something stupid. "Erm, bye, Matt." I give him a small wave and turn around, yanking open the door so hard it slams against the wall.

Chapter Five

My steps are uneven and flighty as I leave, mumbling bye to the other cashiers and holding on tight to my handbag as I push through the doors and out into the small car park in front of the complex.

Out in the sunshine, I take deep breaths and calm my erratic pulse. Never in all my forty years of life have I ever reacted to a male of the species like I have on every occasion with Matt. Not with Ronni and Chrissy's dad, not with the few men I'd managed to be with since him, no one. Matt made my blood churn, my stomach whirl, and my heart race like it was running the Melbourne Cup.

I have to get away from here before my old arse does something stupid like march back in there and kidnap the poor guy. Heading to the car, I spot my girls lazing under the shade of the giant pineapple, sipping their drinks. When they see me, they gather their things and stand, dusting themselves off before beelining to meet me.

"Heads up," I call as I toss the car keys to Ronni. "Where do you want to go now?"

Her smile is huge and lights up the world. "Are you serious, Mum? I get to drive, *and* pick the place?"

I nod, happy to see just how ecstatic she is about the prospect. It's a rare occasion when they get to drive my baby. My gas-guzzling XY is my pride and joy, so it's a treat for them when I relinquish the controls. We cross at the pedestrian overpass to get back to the car, cracking open all the windows to let the heat out.

Absently, I slide into the passenger side, the vinyl searing a path up my backside. With a pained yelp and a little manoeuvring, I have the car seat cover back in place and the comfort increases. I relax in an effort to calm my still-humming body. Handing over control isn't so bad, since the gallery is on the same property as the pineapple and I'm not sure my shaking hands could get us even that short distance safely.

No more than a few minutes later, Ronni is pulling up out the front of the local gallery where she's been hanging to go since we started planning this trip. One of my girls in an artist, the other loves animals. And I just wanted to see the Big Pineapple again.

I still don't know why, don't understand the pull to go there, but if Matt is anything to do with that pull, well....

"Mum! Look at that sculpture. Isn't it amazing?" she gasps excitedly, pointing to a sculpture of... something. I have no idea.

"Go and enjoy it, Ron. Be free, be free!" I tell her, looking forward to taking in the gallery at a more leisurely pace.

Ronni drags her twin sister off to show her everything the gallery has to offer, and I watch them chatting happily as they disappear. The way people can create something from nothing constantly amazes me. I've watched Ronni turn empty toilet roll tubes into mini masterpieces with just a pair of scissors. I've been amazed at the three-dimensional animals she's made from a single piece of A4 paper. Those creations were when she was six years old, and the artistry has improved tenfold over the years.

Allowing the girls their freedom to roam between the gallery and the zoo, I wander off to enjoy the gardens and extensive bushland surrounding the large property. I'm lost in the beauty of the place when I sense a presence nearby. Looking around shows me nothing though, and I go back to admiring the trees. Exciting, I know. But the way Mother Nature has created flora has always fascinated me; she's the original artist.

My hands are enjoying the rough texture of the bark when a set of hands on my hips makes me jump. I try to spin around but lips on my neck stop me, the telltale zing of energy telling me who is behind me. His voice confirms it, the rumble of his baritone zipping straight to my core.

Manoeuvring in his arms, I manage to face him, looking up into those soulful blue eyes of his. They're bright, accentuated by his tanned skin.

"Why me?" I can't help but ask. "With all the beauties you'd get around here, why me? Or are you playing me for a fool because I so obviously come across as desperate." My tone is condescending. No one would ever want me — mother to twin girls of nineteen, rolls of extra skin that have never shifted no matter what I've done, and fatty bits to boot.

He lifts his hand to caress my face, the touch already familiar and soothing. "There's something about you that draws me in. Your daughters are beautiful, but I can see deeper than that. I can see they get their beauty from you."

I'm flattered, but also sceptical. Don't guys just spout lines like this to get laid? It's been so long, I have no idea. Being out of the game for years, and starting off without a clue, has done nothing for my self-esteem or my knowledge. I just feel like I'm being sceptical for no reason, but on the other hand, I don't want to be suckered in by anyone. It makes for a lonely life.

My phone chimes with a text.

Ronni: Mum, where are you? Just want to let you know they're closing at 4.

My fingers swish across the screen.

Me: Be back before then. Just being one with nature.

Ronni: *Eye roll* Meet you back at the car then xxx

Me: Love you too.

I lock the screen and tuck it away in my pocket before looking up at Matt. His attention unnerves me and heats my passion all at the same time. It's confusing to say the least.

"I have to go soon."

When he doesn't answer, I get fidgety. My mother told me not to fidget as it distracted her, but I can't help it; he makes me do it. I'm nervous too, which makes it worse.

"Where do you live? Are you close by?" His voice is low and breathy, and it skims across my cheek as he leans in to my ear. When he finishes his question, he nibbles on my earlobe, sending a trickle of arousal downwards. I can't think, let alone answer as his teeth graze the side of my neck, down farther to my shoulder. That spot in between has me panting with need, a need left untended for too long.

When his hand skims down my body, touching my

mummy tummy, I shy away. I've not been comfortable with that area since the girls were born. He doesn't withdraw his touch though. In fact, I'm pretty sure he moves closer, hand skimming over my tummy and down to the apex of my thighs. The back of my head connects with the tree trunk when I relax involuntarily at his caresses down there.

I hear a moan, and only realise it's my own when his breathy chuckle fans against my neck, cooling the sweaty skin. "You like that?" he whispers in my ear. There are no words, just a noise that vaguely resembles a "Yes."

While I'm distracted by his breath fanning my ear, he slips his hand under my shirt and into the waistband of my stretch pants. My instinct is to pull away, to remove myself from his magic touch, but only because I'm unsure. Of myself, of him, of everything. This right here is foreign to me. My doubting thoughts are cut short when his questing fingers sneak into my knickers to reach my clit, circling it slowly.

His voice is raspy, broken, when he utters a short string of magic words. "Oh my God, you're so wet. I love it." Then he groans when my body responds to his declaration, sending more moisture to my cleft. While his fingers travel to bury in my pussy, his head snuggles into the crook of my shoulder, teeth grazing the skin in rhythm with his fingers.

My hips thrust, the pressure of his thumb on my clit becoming harder with the motion. I don't know how he's managed the angle, but it's perfect. With the next swirl of my pelvis, he hits both pleasure points, inside and out, and I'm suddenly pulsing in his grip, muscles grasping his digits tight. As my contractions subside, with the help of the gentle swish across my sensitive nubbin, he licks up my neck and whispers, "You never answered my question about where you live."

"Down south" is all I can force out of my mouth, brain too far gone with pleasure to think of anything more elaborate.

"I'd love to go 'down south,' but I need to know how far away you live, how far I have to go to see you again." He resumes his nibbles, but his question has doused a large portion of the flames he kindled. My body goes rigid. "What's wrong?"

I can't move my head back to see him, so I just answer, "Adelaide. We live down south, in Adelaide." He reels his head back faster than I'd like.

"Are you serious?" I nod sadly. "How far have you travelled to get here, get to me?"

Unbelievably, his hand is still down my pants, stroking softly as we chat. "We've been on the road for over four weeks. Went on a road trip to see all the big things we could before Ronni and Chrissy start uni next month."

"So," he says, swirling his fingers and thumb again, "how long are you in town for? When do you need to leave?"

I feel tears pushing their way out at his forlorn tone, and I just know that mine will match his. "By the end of the week."

"So soon?" His disappointment is breaking my heart, and the fact that we're leaving just makes the pain worse, which makes no sense. We don't even know each other.

I nod. "It'll take us at least a week to drive back since we'll make a few stops in different towns on the way. Probably take the more direct route across country rather than through the major centres." I'm trying to hold it together, I really am, but this moment we're stuck in is pulling me in opposing directions. "Plus, I'm only on leave from my job for six weeks. After that I need to be back there or risk losing my position."

It's his turn to nod now as he curls his fingers into a fist and withdraws his hand from my pants, tucking my T-shirt back into place on the way out. With a lost expression, he raises his hand to his face. One finger stretches out, reaching towards his mouth. The little-boy-lost look changes the closer the finger gets to his tongue, morphing into rapture when they meet. I can't help but be fascinated as I watch him suck his fingers clean of my juices, amazed that someone would do that.

I told you, my experience with guys is shithouse. I know nothing. Obviously!

His groan and rolled-back eyes tell me that he's enjoying my essence, and it reaches something else within me that I'd rather not acknowledge right now. Something born of deep longing.

When's he's finished licking and sucking his fingers, he caresses my face with the other hand, tracing my cheeks and nose gently. "Before you head home, is it too much to ask for one night with you? May I have a night before you leave?"

It is delivered so sincerely, so passionately, that my only and immediate answer is "Yes."

We exchange phone numbers before walking hand in hand back to my car. I can't help but laugh when his eyes go round at the classic metal muscle my girls are waiting beside. It makes my happiness boundless when my beast is admired. When he's finished drooling over her, much to Ronni's amusement and Chrissy's bemused head shakes, he finishes his circuit of the car and wraps me in his arms. His chin rests on my head for the moment before he dips down to kiss me tenderly.

"See you tonight for dinner, then?" he asks playfully.

With a cheeky grin, I tell him, "I dunno. Maybe we'll go check out somewhere else tonight. Any recommendations?"

"Cheeky. See you later." With another kiss for me and a nod for my twins, he's gone, and I'm left standing there like a lovesick fool until two loud coughs gain my attention.

"You done, Mum? Can we get going now? Everything's closing."

I toss the keys to Chrissy this time, giving her a chance to drive too. I sit and gaze out the windows as we go the short distance back to the caravan park before dinnertime.

Chapter Six

Dinner in the café isn't as stilted as the past two nights, having a better grasp on this flirting thing. Matt sends cheeky grins and winks my way whenever our eyes meet, and I'm pretty sure I've never blushed so much in my life.

When he comes over with the bill at the end of our meal, he taps the paper as he asks, "You free in an hour?" Gorgeous blue eyes sparkle as I glance up, and in that moment of unspoken desire, I feel a boot connect with my shin. Resisting the urge to wince, I nod. His smile is blinding as he taps the paper again. "See you there in an hour, then."

Ronni and Chrissy high-five each other when he goes through the café door, and Chrissy passes a $20 to her sister.

"What the…?"

"We had a bet on when he'd ask you out," Ronni tells me.

"I bet on before dessert."

"And I wagered on after." Ronni smirks as she pockets the note.

Gobsmacked, I mutter, "I can't believe you placed bets on me." I'm still shaking my head at them as we leave, but I'm not too distracted to notice Matt's small smile and the finger tapping his wrist. I push the hair from my eyes as I grin back and nod.

***

Back at the caravan, my girls fuss about in the bedroom whispering to each other. They've done this many times before so I pay them no attention, instead opening an old book I brought with me. I'm enjoying the fluff storyline when they emerge. One look at their expressions tells me they've been up to no good. It's their version of the calm before the storm.

With one eyebrow raised, I assess their demeanour. "Well? What are you two plotting this time?"

Chrissy giggles as they pull their hands from behind their backs.

"Pretty dress. Where are you going?"

"Not us, silly. You. You've got thirty minutes, Mum. Let us doll you up."

I think I'm gaping at them. Like a fish out of water perhaps. No one moves for a good minute as I deem whether or not they're serious.

They are.

I place the book down and shake my head. With a small sigh, I tell them, "All right then. Do your worst."

With gleeful grins and bouncy claps, which make the van rock, they haul me off the couch and start their super-fast makeover.

***

I feel like an idiot as I teeter in heels I'm not used to up to his front door. Hesitantly, I knock, the sound weak even to my ears. My doubts about being here crowd in on me until that door opens and I'm greeted by this heart-stopping, shirtless hunk.

Matt's smile lights up the dark night and my doubts scurry back into the corner where I hope they'll stay. He pushes the door wide for me and gestures inside without moving. His placement has me rubbing against him as I try to walk through.

I swear I hear a hissed inhale too, just before his hand connects with my fleshy arse with a resounding *crack*. I squeak at the unexpected contact, jerking my butt forward. His chuckle ripples through me, a physical reaction that doesn't seem to change.

When the door shuts behind me, I feel the atmosphere change as Matt closes the distance between us. His mouth descends on my shoulder, kissing and nibbling his way to my ear, where he whispers, "You didn't have to get dressed up for me, but I'm sure loving that you did."

The length of his hard cock rubs my lower back and I instinctively push back. His strong arms come around my waist, holding me tight as he grinds against me. A moan escapes and I let my head fall back to rest on his shoulder. Questing hands slide down to my thighs, grasping the dress. Air hits my skin as the fabric is hitched higher. Warm hands caress me, making me burn up inside.

"Oh God."

A growl reverberates on my neck, triggering a rush of wetness to my pink parts. I hear a voice moan Matt's name. *Oh right, that's mine.*

He groans. "Do that again."

"Oh, Matt."

At his name on my lips, he pushes his cock harder against me. The hands under my dress start to wander, caressing my upper thighs and around to the front of my G-string—another of my girls' makeover treats. His fingers find the edge of the fabric and slide beneath.

I'm conscious of my weight as I use him to support

my balance, opening my legs to grant him better access to my pussy. Tension helps keep me upright without leaning too heavily on him, but when he whispers "Relax" in my ear and pulls me closer, I succumb. If he thinks he can handle my heft, then so be it. When he copes just fine with me, I submit to his request.

His strokes through my pussy lips and the pressure of his thumb on my clit take me quickly to orgasm. I'm boneless, leaning to the side on wobbly legs. My panting is all I can hear in the front room of his place.

A kiss placed on my hair makes me feel cherished, although isn't it too soon to be feeling anything but lust?

His husky tone in my ear sends a shiver through me. "Are you cold?"

"Nuh-uh," I reply. "How can I possibly be cold with such heat between us?" *Where the hell did that come from?*

Matt chuckles, rubbing his hands up and down my exposed thighs. "So it was me who made you shiver, then?"

"You'll get a big head making assumptions like that."

"How do you know I haven't already got one?"

Even in my woeful inexperience, I can hear the innuendo-loaded question.

"Ugh." I'm not yet able to produce a coherent sentence though, so I stick with a grunt and add in a moan.

"I know this is quick," he murmurs, "but I need to be inside you."

I nod, knowing he'll feel the motion of my head. In a daze, he moves us through the space until the solid feel of a mattress bumps my knees. I'm spun in his arms until we're facing and he kisses me on the nose before pushing me backwards.

I can't help the squeak that escapes as I hit his bed.

Above me, I admire the surfer-blond god standing over me, muscles accentuated by tanned skin. My fingers itch to touch him and my mouth waters with the need to taste every accessible inch.

"If you keep looking at me like that, it'll be over too soon."

Unsure where the cockiness comes from, I sass, "Could be over before it begins if you keep standing there."

When he doesn't move, I sit up and tuck my finger into the waistband of his shorts. He sucks in a breath at my touch. Matt has no idea how wonderful that small sound is, how much it instils an unheard-of boldness to my next actions. I test the waters by running my fingers lightly up each side, scoring the skin gently with my nails. Looking up at his hiss, I like what's standing before me.

Hooded eyes, head tilted back, and hands fisting at his sides. The sight gives me all I need to go ahead. But my hands give me away as they tickle along the underside of his waistband on the way to the button and fly.

I'm shaking. And he feels it.

Strong hands, larger than mine, cover where they touch him. "Are you okay, Belle?" I nod, but he must see something—probably uncertainty—in my eyes. "Is everything all right? You're shaking."

I swallow, suddenly very doubtful of everything—his attraction to me, my ability to do this, the works. From sure to trembling in less than thirty seconds. Wonderful. I really am a loser.

A quick wriggle loosens my hands from beneath his and I do my best to escape his presence, ending up on the other side of the bed.

Matt speaks as I huddle on his pillow. "At the risk of sounding like a complete idiot, is there something I did wrong?"

I shake my head, unfurling myself enough to pat the pillow beside me. "I must be dysfunctional."

His little laugh, the one that doubts my words, earns him a glare. "Okay, you want to explain why you think that?"

I pat the pillow again. "Have a seat, Matt." When he's comfortable, I begin my story, all the while wishing I just had the confidence to sleep with him instead of boring him to tears with my tale of woe.

I start simple. "To cut to the chase, I'm an epic loser. I have no clue about men and never did." I pause for a second, wondering if I should keep going. A gentle squeeze of my fingers makes me glance up into the most beautiful set of cerulean eyes I've ever seen, and the compassion in them melts my heart. Maybe just softens it a little then.

I take a deep breath.

Chapter Seven

"I vowed not to be a virgin by my twenty-first birthday." I sigh. "With that stupid vow came the predators. It was almost as if they could smell my loneliness and desperation on me, kind of like a lion smells fear. I'm guessing you'd know of the type, they wine, dine, they sixty-ahem… you know."

He nods solemnly as I continue. "Anyway, one of them found me wallowing in a pool of self-pity one night and schmoozed his way into my life. Six months later, after wheedling his way into my dreams and knickers, I was pregnant, ecstatic, and expecting promises of forever from him." I make a buzzer noise and snort. "Boy, was I ever wrong.

"Knocked up, dumped, and heartbroken wasn't good enough for the universe to saddle me with. When I found out I was expecting twins, I went on a downhill slide."

His fingers wrap around mine, bringing me back from reminiscing hell. "Didn't you have anyone to help you?"

"Only my dad. I bunked in his bungalow after giving up my room at uni and the last six months of study."

Matt's calming circles widen as my breath hitches. "Was there any way to finish off the year?"

I shake my head. "Matt, emotionally, I hit rock bottom. Only the fact that I had a roof over my head stopped me from being homeless. But only for a little while."

The circles with his palm slow, drawing out the time it takes to do a full circuit of my back. With a deep breath, I continue, "A week before I gave birth, he kicked me out. Told me that his girlfriend's teenage daughter needed the space more than me."

I swear, it's at this point that Matt actually starts growling. "What an arsehole thing to do."

I shrug. "I could never prove it, but I'm positive it was the girlfriend's brainwashing that made him do it. She claimed her pussy was gold." Matt chuckles at this. "I got the last laugh though. I got his car and she ended up with nothing but a barren piece of land and a condemned house."

"So what did you do?"

"One of the girls who used to wax lyrical about her ah-ma-zing boyfriend in high school ended up pregnant, dumped, and pacing the halls of the same maternity ward as me. We rekindled a friendship over a mutual dislike of baby poo and shared a house for many years. Her and her boy, me and my girls. All went great for ages."

"But? What happened?"

"They grew up. Puberty hit, something changed between the three of them. They went from being the best of friends and living in each other's pockets to not being able to look each other in the eye. No one would explain what had happened, so Vicky took her boy and they moved out. Never saw them again."

"Have the girls ever said why?"

I shake my head. "Nope. Don't expect them to either. But a positive came from it. They know more about sex now than I ever did, and I can't find fault in that. If it stops them from being the idiot I was, then that's good."

"But if you hadn't been an idiot, then you wouldn't

have them, would you?"

"True, but I always wonder what could've been."

Silence falls between us.

Matt breaks it. "Their confidence shows though. No matter what else happened, I think you did good with them."

I duck my head, embarrassed at the compliment. "Thanks."

A finger comes under my chin, lifting gently until our eyes meet. I think that's sincerity there as he tells me, "Don't shy away from me. I'm telling it to you straight." He kisses my nose and moves down to my lips. I must be in shock as I sit and wonder why the hell he's kissing me. I frown when he stops and leans back.

"What's the matter, Belle?"

"Why are you kissing me?" I'm honestly confused. "Why aren't you running for the hills and kicking me out of your house?"

His forehead meets mine when he lowers his head, eyes too close to focus comfortably. "Why would I run? Why would I kick you out?"

"Because I'm a pathetic loser who has twin teens and can count on one hand the number of sexual encounters in twenty years. Add to that, this" —I motion to my body— "astounding figure, and I can't understand what you're doing here." I push up off the bed. "I don't know what I'm doing here."

Panic at making a fool of myself claws up my throat until a large hand grabs my arse cheek. The shock is enough to shake me out of it.

"I can't put into words what you do to me or why I want you here, but will you let me show you?"

I hesitate, assessing those baby blues. The nod is easy, surprisingly so.

His kisses are slow, tender, thoughtful even as he takes my mouth with his. This business of taking one's time for a kiss is new to me and I think I like it. Come to think of it, I believe I'd like any style and speed of kiss Matt gives me.

Our tongues parry in the combined space of our mouths, but it's not enough. I want more. I'm over being the hard-working wall flower who has no life of her own. I want to live. Want to experience. And I want to do so many naughty, dirty things to this gorgeous man.

My heart rate picks up as I take the initiative and deepen our kiss. It feels a little weird to be the one taking control, but I like it. even if it doesn't last for long. Matt grasps my hips and drags me back onto the bed where he's kneeling.

As my feet hit the edge of the mattress, the impact against the side knocks my heels to the floor. They land with a solid thud. Their noise breaks some kind of spell and Matt stops. Eye to eye, I can see his pupils have blown out, the widest I've ever seen them. Without breaking our staring match, he runs his hands all over me, tickling, caressing, oh… searching for the zipper.

The sound of him pulling it down is loud in the small bedroom. The night air chills my overheated skin as he pulls my dress off over my head. As soon as there's bared skin, he seems to lose the iron control he had thirty seconds ago. As his questing fingers explore my padded frame, mine delve into the open front of his shorts. I must gasp when my hands wrap around his cock, as a rumbling laugh vibrates through his body. His eyes crinkle with his smile.

I murmur, "Seriously? Awesome." I can't even get my fingers to meet when I try to circle his girth. This is a good thing. This is the stuff of dirty books and Tumblr posts.

I push his shorts down until his fat cock springs free into my waiting hands. Caressing its length, I enjoy the silky-smooth texture in my palms. His groans speak to me, telling me what I need to know. Somehow I've made this man hard, and despite all my doubts and insecurities, I'm ready to do this.

With one hand grasping his length, I use my other hand to push his shorts all the way to his knees. Seeing his completely naked body, I fight the urge to cover myself, my inadequacy in comparison to his perfectly sculpted form is glaringly obvious. My arms are halfway across my torso when they're stopped.

"Don't." His tone is gentle, but the word is most definitely a command. He holds my arms away from my body and runs his gaze up and down. Everywhere Matt's eyes land, tingles spring up until I'm humming with arousal. How quickly can this man change my reactions? Matt releases one arm and runs his hand across my tummy, the same touch that made me shy away from him earlier. "You don't get how beautiful you are, do you? No concept that this here" — he rubs my belly — "is proof of the lives you brought into the world. You should be proud of it."

I'm speechless and I can feel the prickling in my eyes at his kind words. There's no chance to reflect any further as his hand still grasping my arm pulls it behind my back and yanks me close to him. Matt's mouth descends on mine, his tongue exploring thoroughly.

The sensation of slowly falling has me gripping his shoulder with my free hand as he lowers me to the bed. Following me down, Matt releases my arm and rests his hands on either side of my head, his weight pressing slightly. It's been so long since I experienced the glide of skin on skin. While I'm daydreaming about how good this is, Matt's retrieved a condom from somewhere and is kneeling between my thighs.

I'm fascinated by the way the latex stretches as he rolls it on, and I swear my mouth is watering at the thought of fitting that thing between my lips. But later. Pussy first.

In an unexpected burst of boldness, I reach down and rub my fingers through my juices, spreading the lips apart, waiting for him. With a groan, Matt lines up his cock and pushes forward slowly. This is heaven! I never thought I'd want to feel like a virgin again, but the way he stretches me makes it seem like it.

"Oh my God," I groan. "More, Matt. I want to feel it all."

Unable to wait for his torturously slow motion, I lift my legs and lock them around his hips. Heels digging into his butt, I push down, forcing him inside me faster. My back arches as he bottoms out, pleasure zinging through me. Pulling out slowly, he thrusts back in, and so it begins.

Pressure builds with each push and pull, the sheer width of him rubbing against every spot within me, bringing me closer to orgasm. Nothing can compare to the way my body explodes and the way my pussy grasps his cock so fiercely.

I'm still shuddering beneath him when he grunts on one last push. It's amazing and rather new that I can feel his cock pulsing when he comes. Instead of withdrawing straight away, which has been the sum of the few experiences before, he drops his head to my shoulder and exhales roughly.

"Fuck. That was awesome."

I can't help the chuckle at having sex deemed

awesome. I'm kind of chuffed by it, to tell the truth.

"You know, laughing after mind-blowing sex has the potential to damage egos."

My laughter separates us as I reach up to stroke a finger along his jaw line. "I was just thinking that awesome is new and a 100-percent improvement on 'thanks for that' or 'perhaps we'll catch up again' that I've heard in the past."

Matt shakes his head. "I can't believe no one else recognised the treasure you are." He grins. "But then that's good for me."

After disposing of the condom, Matt acts as a big spoon, curling himself behind me. His comfort, his heat, and the way his chin rests on my head lulls me off to sleep easily.

Chapter Eight

The chime of my phone rouses me from slumber. I'm surprised to feel a warm body behind me and to see the sun peeking in through curtains. There's no stopping the grin that spreads across my face as Matt moves behind me, pressing his morning wood against my backside. I wriggle around until it slips between my legs, sliding easily in my slick heat. The head nudges my opening and I think nothing of it to push down.

I'm enjoying my stolen moment of bliss until my bladder reminds me of more urgent matters. Reluctantly I slide out of bed and go off to find the bathroom and my phone.

There's a bunch of notifications, including three missed messages from Chrissy.

9:00 p.m. Chrissy: Are you staying there tonight?

11:37 p.m. Chrissy: Guessing you're sleeping over.

7:49 a.m. Chrissy: We're going to explore the town on foot today. Relax and have fun. Xxx

I text back, fingers flying over the screen.

Me: Have fun, girls. I'll be back later. Xxx

I pad quietly back to bed, sliding in next to Matt. His cock is still hard, so I take it in my hand and pump slowly. He wakes gradually, groaning as he moves his hips in time.

"Good morning, gorgeous."

I blush at the endearment. "Good morning to you." I give his length a squeeze. "Waking up happy, I see."

His eyes open slowly until they meet mine. "Waking up like this every morning would make me extremely happy." Arching backwards so his dick is still in my hand, Matt manages to reach into the bedside drawer and retrieve a condom. With a smile, he passes it to me. "Care to do the honours?"

***

At least two hours and a growing pile of wrappers later, we're up, showered, dressed, and eating in his small kitchen. As I pick up my phone, my finger slips on the camera icon, opening the app. Without thinking, I raise it and snap a few pictures of Matt. One of them catches him midchew and he protests, trying to grapple the phone from my hand. I'm laughing so hard at his objection that he manages to snag it from my weak grip and starts scrolling through the photos.

Gasping for air, I manage a "Don't delete them!"

Instead of erasing them, he slides closer to me and holds up the phone, aiming it our way. "Smile, sugar."

I roll my eyes just as he takes the pic, and he keeps tapping that damn button as I pull faces at him. He even turns my face to his and snaps pictures as he kisses me.

The kiss deepens and the phone is forgotten. When a piece of his cereal ends up in my mouth, I pull away, laughing. I stick out my tongue with the rogue grain on the end and give it back to him.

Sexy moment broken, he picks up the phone to look

through the gallery. I have to laugh at the silly faces, and secretly sigh over the one of us kissing. With a few taps, he says, "I need a copy," then keeps scrolling.

He comments on the photos as he scrolls, but something renders him silent. I glance over at him and then the screen.

"Why are they standing next to a giant poo?"

I snort, then laugh, almost choking on my juice. "Our trip has been all about Australia's big things. That was taken in Kiama."

He continues to scroll, laughing at Ronni's expression when she first approached the giant piece of excrement. When he gets to the banana, I tell him, "That was at Coffs Harbour. And oh my God, you should've heard the filth they were spouting there." He flicked to the next image of the girls' rude gestures. "And at Wauchope...."

Matt laughs. "The bull! Big balls comments, am I right?"

I nod, putting on the face of unimpressed mum. This just makes him laugh harder.

Together we revisit my holiday in reverse order, until we get to the first photo I took of Ronni trying to take a peek up the kilt of the Big Scotsman in Adelaide. When he asks where that is, his face falls. It's so far away from here.

Matt scrolls back up to the ones of us together and puts the phone down. His arm curls around my shoulder and he pulls me close, planting a kiss on my head. We stay like that a little while until he declares, "Let's enjoy the time we have together, then. There's a town to explore."

***

There's a certain comfort in having my hand held as we walk through town, even if it is completely foreign to me. On the way, we run into Chrissy waiting outside a shop, so when Ronni exits the store, the four of us continue together.

By mid-afternoon, we're ready to hide in the shade. Back at Matt's, I grab my keys and open the car to air out. As I'm hugging him goodbye and making plans to catch up at his work tonight, his landline rings. He releases me with "I'll see you tonight" as he darts inside.

"We'll be there!"

He blows me a kiss as the door closes, leaving us in his driveway.

"Let's go, lovelies. We'll hit up the ice-cream shop on the way back to the van."

***

At dinnertime, Matt's not there and we're served by someone new. On the way back to the van, I stop past his place to touch base with him, but the house is dark and no one answers. I call his mobile, but get no response there either. Attempting to wear a brave and unaffected mask, I take us to the caravan and spend the evening finding out about the twins' day.

In the back of my mind nags the horrid little voice telling me I've been duped.

We have two days left here before we have to leave, and I won't bring their holiday down by being a sad sack. My mood barely improves by morning, but I'm determined to let them enjoy what's left of our break. I indulge Ronni in whatever else she wants to do, and the day after that we do what Chrissy wants to do.

Both nights we dine at the café, and both nights I suffer without Matt there. I ask another of the waitstaff, but no one knows where he is. Even worse than that, the young woman I have the misfortune of asking gives me a look as if to tell me I'm not worthy of his time, even if he were here.

That crushes my spirit completely. I feel used and taken for a fool. This is not the way I want to feel at all. So the following morning when we need to leave, I pack us up with a forced smile on my lips and get on the road.

Ronni's in the back seat through this leg of the trip, playing with my phone when a message comes through.

"Who's that?"

Silence.

"Ronni, who's messaging?"

"Just a telemarketer, Mum."

I glance at her in the rear-view mirror and shrug. That shit wastes my time.

It takes four days to get home; the desire to take our time and explore each town has left us all and the consensus is to just get home and start fresh. Starting uni after taking a gap year is becoming a reality for them, and I no longer seem to have the drive to do what I've done for so many years.

As a personal assistant to a CEO, there are long hours, demanding bosses, and a to-do list longer than I am tall. Even though I haven't heard from Matt since he blew me a kiss at his front door, Adelaide no longer holds my attention. After a taste of what's out there, I find I want more than being stuck in an office from dawn to dusk.

Despite not wanting it to, my mind keeps skipping to my delectable waiter and the short time we spent together.

***

When I step back into the office on Monday morning, the first place I go is the boss's office to hand in my resignation. For no one other than me, my life is going to change. When they can't convince me to stay, management organises an advert for the job and I begin to make a comprehensive list of everything my job entails.

By the end of the day, I'm exhausted. On my way back to the car, my phone rings. On seeing the screen, I hesitate. The ringing stops and then starts up again. This time I pick it up.

"Hey, Belle." He sounds so damn sad.

"Matt, are you all right?"

"Not really. That call I went inside for was my mum telling me my grandma had died. I left straight after the call."

My heart breaks for him. "Oh, Matt. I'm so sorry."

"Thanks, Belle. Just hearing your voice makes me feel better. I could've done with you this past week."

"Why didn't you call me, then?"

"I drove three hours to be with family, and it wasn't till I went to call you that I realised I'd left my damn phone at home."

After his explanation and sincere-sounding apologies, we hang up. My step is lighter as I go to the car.

With no time to talk on Tuesday, Matt stalks me via text, sending me funny memes and things that brighten my stress-filled day.

By the weekend, we've managed to have a conversation or two, but they're both cut short. Saturday and Sunday are his super-busy days at both the pineapple and the café, so brief late-night calls suffice. By the end of the second week back to the daily grind, I'm completely over it all. The sporadic contact with Matt is keeping my positive thoughts intact, but I'm missing his smile and touch so badly. The urge to jump in my car and drive till I reach him is so strong.

But I can't.

Ronni starts university in two weeks, and Chrissy starts her internship with the Adelaide Zoo and Monarto Open Range in a few days. I have no intention of disrupting their lives just so I can move, but each day I'm without his smile, his voice, and his touch is another day I go slowly insane.

Chapter Nine

I want him with a passion I never expected to feel, never thought someone else could feel for me. People do long-distance relationships, and I have no clue how they manage it. I am going nuts.

At the end of another short call, he clears his throat a few times to break the quiet, umming and ahhing.

"Would you ever move up to Queensland?" he enquires softly.

This takes balls to ask, and I honestly don't think he would have if there wasn't something there from his side. I'd move there for sure, but many things would need to be sorted first.

"In a heartbeat, but it would take me a good six months to tie all the loose ends and be able to move." I let him absorb that for moment before I ask, "Would you ever move to South Australia?"

I'm going to take his silence as contemplative, rather than stage fright or the phone equivalent. "Yeah, I would. But like you, things would need to be tied up first. Jobs, house, and all the little things."

When tonight's phone call is over, I curl up on my favourite seat of the couch. Dreams of Matt fill my mind, so I'm suitably annoyed when Chrissy wakes me from slumber, her voice high-pitched and urgent.

"Mum! Wake up, please, wake up!" The frantic tone in her voice triggers my motherly instincts and within seconds, I'm awake, looking around the room with bleary eyes for a fire or flood or something else catastrophic. When I focus on her face, the expression there doesn't quite match the urgency in her tone.

"What's up, Chrissy? Where's the fire?"

For a second, it slips, and I see excitement sneak through the cracks in her façade.

"What's going on? I saw that smile you're trying to hide."

She reaches down and yanks me forcibly off the couch, pulling me down the hall to the front door. A frown dips my brows. I'm so confused. It's like she's kicking me out of my own home!

As we near the front door, I see a pile of luggage near Ronni, who's placing her bag on the side table. "Where are you going?" I ask her, more confused now than a minute ago.

"Nowhere if I have a choice," replies a voice I dream of every night.

"Matt?" It comes out as a choked whisper. I must be dreaming still. He's not standing in my front entryway, appearing from behind Ronni. Disbelief is written all over me, and it's not until he approaches, eyes locked to mine, that I start to believe this is a dream. Dream come true perhaps as he wraps me in his strong embrace and squeezes me for all he's worth.

Tears hit his T-shirt as I cry with sheer happiness that he's here, in my house, in my state, and hopefully, in my life.

I hear Chrissy and Ronni retreat to their rooms, leaving us alone.

Matt strokes the hair from my face, cupping my cheeks with his hands. His lips meet my forehead in a kiss that makes my insides melt and my knees go weak. Staring up at him through teary eyes, I study every detail of his face, his ocean-blue eyes, the scruffy stubble on his cheeks and chin, the sun-bleached blond hair sticking out from his head like he's been running his hands through it constantly.

"How…? Why…? Talk to me."

"I think Ronni's been a bit concerned." He smiles down at me. "She's been… um… messaging me since before you got back."

"Ronni!" I yell as jealousy and shock zip through me. Matt must see it in my eyes because his palms are suddenly firmer on my face, and his eyes are blazing.

"She replied to my text when you were on the road and it was meant to be a surprise, but when she told me you were so sad, that's when I rang you. She's been doing what she can to get me down here faster. I'm here for *you* and no one else. You should be thanking your daughter, not envying her." His little chuckle should piss me off, but it doesn't. It just makes me crave him more, makes me realise how much I've missed his smile, his eyes, and his chuckle.

I reach up and run my fingers through the tangled mess, massaging his scalp as I go. Unable to maintain this distance, I grip his hair, bringing his face in line with mine. The kiss starts off gentle, the reacquainting of two souls, but then the embers ignite, catching quickly on the bone-dry tinder of time apart. Together we create a flash fire of desire, burning hotter than it did when we met.

Before I disrobe us both at the front door, I walk us sideways into my bedroom, conveniently located a few feet away from our current location, kicking the door shut behind us.

When the meeting of flesh occurs, it's equivalent to all the very best fireworks descriptions I've ever read. The epic sensations caused by his thrust and retreat make stars appear before my eyes, and the heavens should be singing his praises right now.

This is my perception of love. The connection of souls whose need to be together overrides distance, circumstance, and age. The knowledge that the other will go to whatever lengths they can for their beloved. And of course, the explosive sex that glues them even more securely.

So when his hard and deep thrusts while biting my neck cause me to convulse in the best orgasm ever, I declare my affection for him rather loudly. "Fuck, I love you!"

In the afterglow as my body lies like a limp noodle on my bed, sweaty and thoroughly exhausted, Matt curls himself around me and trails patterns over my skin with his fingers.

"Did you mean it?" he asks, a touch of uncertainty in his voice. I don't need to ask what he means, so I nod.

Meeting his gaze, I raise my hand to his cheek and cup it. "Yes, I meant every yelled word. I've never been so sure about something since the girls were born and I knew without a doubt that I'd love them to the end of time."

"I know it hasn't been long, and some would say it's way too fast, but I love you too, Belle. More than I thought was possible."

The next kiss is full of promises: hot nights, snuggles, support, Christmases, birthdays, and so much more. Of everything you could ever want in a partnership.

But there's one thought that pops into my mind as we're lying comfortably pretzelled in each other's arms. My eyes widen and my mouth gapes open in surprise at the question I haven't asked before now.

"How old are you?"

THE END

About the Author

As a former covert operative, Aria Peyton has jumped from helicopters, commando crawled across enemy lines without underwear, created secret alliances with the things that go bump in the night, and bungee jumped off the top of a Styrofoam factory into a vat of beanbag filler.

With the aid of the Secret Agent Protection Group, she currently masquerades as an average parent, but can leap Lego towers in a single bound, pack school lunches like a boss, and can burn herself on any hot surface without the aid of a how-to manual. Her multiskilling talent is now known throughout the universe.
Never be fooled by the apparent mediocrity though. To do so is at your own peril.

Thank you so much for reading my book. I hope you enjoyed it! I'd love for you to leave a review if you did; reviews are important for all authors.
If you want to stay up-to-date with what's going on with future releases, please check out the following:

Website:
www.ariapeytonauthor.weebly.com

Facebook:
www.facebook.com/authorariapeyton

Instagram:
@authorariapeyton

You can sign up for my newsletter on my website, which is totally non-spammy and highly recommended!

I'd love to hear from you, so please feel free to send me a message on FB, or email
authorariapeyton@gmail.com

Keep reading for an excerpt from
Southern Dreams…

Prologue

The phone rings, flashing *Matt* across the screen. I answer it with a smile on my lips. My best mate went walkabout a week ago and this is the first I've heard from him.

"Matty! How you doing?" I greet cheerily, not bothering to hide the grin in my voice.

"Travis! I'm so good, buddy." There's a brief pause and he says, "I found her."

"That's great, man. I'm so glad you tracked her down. You were a miserable cunt when she left." I chuckle, knowing how true it is. "So, when are you bringing her home?"

There's another pause and I can almost see him scrubbing at the back of his neck. I've known this bloke for pretty much our whole lives, and this kind of silence usually has him reaching for his neck. The hairs on mine go up as the silence drags out.

"I'm staying here." He sighs. "Her girls are in uni and her job is stable, and even though she was ready to pick up and come north when I arrived, leave the house with her girls, I really want to see how we go here first."

I can't even think of what to say. I'm super happy that he's found Belle, and the smile I can hear in his voice is a complete one-eighty from a few weeks ago, but…. We've been in each other's pockets since we were in nappies and it's a shock to know he won't be back any time soon. He could be three states away or on the other side of the world, the reality is still the same.

My best mate isn't coming home.

The silence becomes awkward, and his tone is hesitant. "You okay, Trav?"

"Yeah, I'll be fine." It's embarrassing the way my voice cracks on me, and I can't even hide it. I clear my throat and try again, injecting more humour into my voice. "I'll be fine, Matt. You know me. Pick up and keep going. We'll miss you here though." My chuckle is weak, just like I'm feeling. "I'll miss ya, you lousy fuck." I force a laugh to lighten my morose mood. "You're a bastard, you know that? You've up and left me with the useless pricks here and no one to pick on them with. Who'm I gonna drink beers with now?"

"You've still got Mal and Kayle. I haven't left you completely high and dry."

"Kayle's a knob and you know it! And Mal has Shez to keep him company. They've got their own lives. They're not going to be here every day to entertain me."

He's silent for a moment. "I know, Trav. I just… I need to see where this could go, ya know?"

"I hear ya. Try and visit soon though, yeah?"

"Will do."

We chat for a bit longer before a cheerful female voice in the background calls out "Hi!" and Matt promises to call again soon. When we hang up, I stare at the dark screen and take a moment to breathe. For twenty-six years he's been by my side—brothers in arms, musketeers, the other third of our mischief-making trio. School, sports, camps, and even some workplaces, he's been there for them all. Every up and down. All the good times and bad. If best mates could be soulmates, he'd be mine.

And I'm not ashamed to admit, I'm suddenly feeling

really fucking lost without him. I let my phone drop to the couch and leave it there while I go to the floor-to-ceiling windows that span the width of my lounge room. The view over the valley is superb, and the balcony on the other side of the glass holds a million memories — all involving Matt and our endless hours of chats and quite often, beers. It won't be the same without him here, but I guess I'll adjust. Eventually.

Deep in the heart of me though, I'm not so sure.